This book is dedicated to all the musicians, conductors, narrators, collaborators, technicians and organisers and others who have supported me in my quest to bring music to life for children, with illustrated concerts. You are many and we are a team. In particular I want to thank conductor Robin Browning, and the de Havilland Philharmonic, who first set the ball rolling; Britten Sinfonia, Royal Scottish National Orchestra, BBC National Orchestra of Wales, Royal Liverpool Philharmonic Orchestra, London Mozart Players, Ulster Orchestra, King Edward School Symphony Orchestra, Sheffield Philharmonic Orchestra, Saffron Walden Symphony Orchestra; conductors Gemma New, Ellie Slorach, George Morton, Thomas Blunt, Rebecca Tong, Martin Leigh, Richard Hull, James Burton; and narrators Simon Callow, Polly Ives, Zeb Soanes and Floella Benjamin.

Lastly, a special mention to Siu Chui Li (piano) and Alex Redington (violin) for our *A Brush With Music* adventures. This book wouldn't exist without you all - thank you!

And... to my son, Gabriel... All The Planets x

ACKNOWLEDGEMENTS
Sincere thanks to Janetta Otter-Barry for publishing this book
and Andrew Watson for designing it so beautifully.

Text and illustrations copyright © James Mayhew 2024

Designed by Andrew Watson

The right of James Mayhew to be identified as the author and illustrator of this work has been asserted
by him in accordance with the Copyright, Designs and Patents Act, 1988 (United Kingdom).
First published in Great Britain in 2024 by Otter-Barry Books,
Little Orchard, Burley Gate, Herefordshire, HR1 3QS
www.otterbarrybooks.com

All rights reserved

A catalogue record for this book is available from the British Library

ISBN 978-1-915659-34-7

Illustrated with collage and mixed media

Set in Blacker Pro Text

Printed in Turkey

1 3 5 7 9 8 6 4 2

A Symphony of STORIES

Musical Myths and Tuneful Tales

JAMES MAYHEW

Otter-Barry BOOKS

www.otterbarrybooks.com

CONTENTS

Introduction	7
The Carnival of the Animals	9
The Four Seasons	27
The Sunken Cathedral	41
The Planets	51
The Butterfly Lovers	67
The Firebird	77
Musical Notes	88
Recommended Recordings	92

 # INTRODUCTION

Welcome to *A Symphony of Stories – Musical Myths and Tuneful Tales!*

'Symphony' means 'sounds in harmony' and usually refers to a big piece of music, often divided into four separate parts or 'movements'. But it can also mean a harmonious gathering of themes – and that is what I hope I've created in this set of six musical myths and tuneful tales – a symphony of stories!

Each is inspired by a wonderful piece of music. You will meet the magnificent Firebird, the spectacular Planets, and two young Chinese lovers. You'll see a city sink into the sea, stroll through the seasons in Italy, and march with an amazing animal parade.

Most of the stories are retold from the original tales that inspired the composer. There are dramatic and exciting tales, like *The Sunken Cathedral,* or beautiful and sad stories, like *The Butterfly Lovers*. And some, like *The Firebird*, have wonderful, happy endings.

There are other stories, like *The Carnival of the Animals*, that describe the funny and strange creatures the composer imagined in music, *The Planets*, in which we meet Roman gods, or *The Four Seasons*, where we meet the composer himself!

The composers of the music come from Britain, China, France, Italy and Russia, and their music comes in many shapes and forms, some short, some long. There are pieces written for big orchestras, and others for small ensembles. Some works are collections of short pieces, called suites. They are quite long when heard all together, but you don't have to listen to all of them at once. You could start with just one of Vivaldi's *Seasons*, or perhaps a couple of Holst's *Planets*.

All the music is really easy to listen to, wherever you stream your music. Or, if you are very lucky, you may one day get to hear some of these fabulous compositions in a live concert.

I hope you'll find the stories in this book – and the music they inspired – as magical and unforgettable as I do. And now – the orchestra is all tuned up. Are you ready?

Off we go!

James Mayhew

James Mayhew

THE CARNIVAL OF THE ANIMALS

Music by Camille Saint-Saëns

Roll up! Roll up!

The Carnival was in town and an audience gathered. Music was playing… it was growing louder and louder. Someone was coming, leading the parade. A figure in grand clothes appeared, with long golden hair. He spoke in a roar…

*Let me introduce myself
You're in for quite a feast
With me, the handsome lion
I'm the king of all the beasts.*

*Now meet my menagerie
My friends with teeth and claws
A Carnival of Animals
With wings and tails and paws.*

What a way to start the show
With someone who is known to crow
With crests of red and golden feathers
In and out in all the weathers.

And now the hens join in the fun
Basking in the midday sun
Until it's time to nestle down
And lay their eggs both red and brown.

Gallopy-galloping all of the day
In the desert they frolic and play
Far across the prairie wide
Goofy-toothed and marble-eyed.

They pound their hooves and flick their tails
And chase each other on dusty trails
With tails cut short and ears grown long
Catch a glimpse before they're gone!

*I think it would be hard to feature
A slower kind of little creature...
Everywhere they like to roam
They take along their Home Sweet Home.*

*But if they hear loud shouts or roars
They tend to hide away indoors
And all throughout the winter deep
They'll stay inside their house to sleep.*

THE ELEPHANT

And now it's time for you to meet
An extraordinary creature
Her nose, I think you will agree
Is her identifying feature.

Elegant, majestic
And maybe, just, perchance
This pachyderm is wishing
She could join in with a dance.

Related to the bandicoots
Meet the cousin of the numbat
Acquainted with the wallabies
And best friends with the wombat.

Faster than a boomerang
Leaping like a rocket
And all the time, she's keeping Joey
Safe inside her pocket.

Iridescent colours flash
Little flecks of silver dash
Fishes hide and gently glow
Drifting on the ebb and flow.

CHARACTERS WITH LONG EARS

Oh no, I'm sorry, this is tricky
I don't know what to say!
I think the man who wrote the music
Liked to joke and play.

The sounds you'll hear are very odd
Let's see what next appears
As we listen to the sounds
Of characters with... long ears!

And now here's someone very shy
Hiding in the trees
His song is like an echo
Carried on the breeze.

He calls out here, he calls out there
And so repeats his song
His voice so clear, he sounds so near
But when you look... he's gone!

THE CUCKOO IN THE DEPTHS OF THE WOOD

THE AVIARY

Swooping, diving, gathering
They chatter and they sing
Songs of far-off islands
And songs of taking wing.

*I think perhaps they dream of flying
Far across the sea
Far away from gilded cages
To where they can be free.*

Far below us, deep in rocks
Lie creatures ancient, old
Long extinct and hard to find
Completely dead and cold.

Here lie monsters, sleeping giants
Riddles made of bone
Jumbled up beneath the ground
And petrified in stone.

She glides above her own reflection
Mirrored in the lake
She leaves a trail of broken starlight
Dancing in her wake...

And then the amazing parade was at an end. The lion turned to the audience and waved his paw...

And so the carnival is over
It's time to leave you now
Farewell, so long, give us a cheer
As we take our final bow.

From elephants to kangaroos
With fish ... and birds that fly
To little tortoises and swans
We bid you all...

GOODBYE!

THE FOUR SEASONS

*Music by Antonio Vivaldi
after Sonnets attributed to the composer*

SPRING

*With joyous birdsong, behold the Spring
The sky rejoices, filled with gold!
The gentle Zephyr stirs the trees
By banishing the cold.*

Golden and warm, in a sky tumbled with cloud, the sun appeared! The gentle breeze blew across the plains, stroking the fresh new grass, carrying birds high and low, spinning and twirling, returning home to remembered nests, so happy to be free from Winter's cold winds.

Antonio strolled through the fields. It was so different from life in the city and he looked forward to a year in the country. He put his hand in his pocket and took out some papers. He was a composer, and he was trying to write a new work, a violin concerto. It was to be something special and different. But the notes just wouldn't come...

He saw a distant shepherd, with his dog by his side, watching the sheep with a keen eye, the ewes round with soon-to-be-born lambs. Antonio waved and the shepherd boy raised his straw hat.

Lying on the sweet grass, under that great sky, the Earth bursting with life, Antonio listened to the birdsong and the trickling brook. Above him, the trees were heavy with swollen buds and blossoms. It seemed as though the leaves unfurled before his eyes, reaching up to greet the sun. The scent of blossoms and bright new flowers filled the air. Could any other season be as beautiful as Spring?

There was a faraway rumble of thunder over the hills, and the dog barked. The breeze was strong and Antonio felt a few passing raindrops. But the sun soon returned.

He closed his eyes and listened as the shepherd boy played his pipe. Ideas for his concerto came and went in the air, joining together with birdsong, as if all the world was in harmony. Could he capture that in music?

"I must try," said Antonio to himself.

SUMMER

A cuckoo in the dusty pine trees
Is singing to the sleepy dove
Summertime is hot and harsh
As storm clouds gather far above.

It was Summer and the crops were swelling, burnished by the sun. Antonio stayed in the shady olive groves, but even so, he could feel the scorching heat. It was really too hot. He wandered down to the brook and saw it had dried right up and the bleached ground was cracked and split. The air was still, sticky and humid. The air was full of mosquitoes and flies, buzzing in annoying circles.

Antonio took out paper and wrote down a few notes. But the flies

wouldn't leave him alone, although he noticed they had a music of their own.

The shepherd boy came and sat next to him, his dog panting at his side.

"What are you writing?" he asked. "I can't read."

"Well, this is music," said Antonio. "I'm trying to capture the Summer with musical notes."

"I think there might be a storm," said the boy. "Can you put that in your music?"

Antonio looked up. The sky was hazy now – and the air felt heavy.

It was as if the valley was holding its breath, waiting for something to happen.

The cuckoo's song sounded like a warning, and in a rush of wind, a storm came tearing through the trees. Thunder and lightning shook the sky, and then came hailstones – hard balls of ice falling from the sky.

The shepherd wept to see the flattened fields of corn.

"Everything's ruined," he cried, as his dog licked his hand.

Antonio looked at his papers – all his inky notes were wet and smudged. "Me too, my friend," he said. "Come on, let's shelter under the pines."

They ran for cover and waited for the storm to pass.

AUTUMN

The air is cooler; Summer's gone
Trees turn gold, glowing bright
The harvesters begin their work
Leaves fall in the Autumn light.

Fruits glowed red, olives ripened, green and black, with grapes sweet for the picking. It was still hot, but there was a gentle breeze as Summer slipped into Autumn.

A walk in the country was a pleasure now. The workers rose with the sun, before it got too hot, gathering grapes from vines and carrying them to huge vats for treading. Antonio loved to watch them stamping the grapes with their bare feet, in a steady rhythm – like another kind of music. It was hard work, but soon the grape juice was collected, ready to make wine.

Now the days grew colder. Antonio wrapped himself in his cloak as he wandered in the cool, misty valley, under golden leaves. He watched the shepherd boy lifting crops onto carts which were pulled away by lumbering horses. The first wine was ready now, and they all shared a cup or two, laughing, tired but happy that the harvest was in.

Antonio turned memories into music, painting scenes with his melodies. When the hunters went by, with their bright, gleaming horns, he wrote those notes down too, even the sound of barking dogs as they ran ahead of the horses.

In the pine trees the hunters spotted a stag.

"Go on, hide," whispered Antonio, and he shooed away the noble beast with his hands. The stag ran off, wide-eyed and elegant, just as the hunters arrived.

Their guns blazed, and Antonio looked away, saddened as the stag stumbled and fell...

He was glad to see the hunters leave, and to have the peace and solitude of the valley once more. He lingered to enjoy the last warm days, for he knew it would soon be cold.

WINTER

Winter's wind is biting cold
And with it brings the swirling snows
All is wrapped in silent white
Now Nature wears her Winter clothes.

Where the crops once grew, all was frozen, and the brook was a sheet of ice. Wrapped in his warmest cape, Antonio waved to the shepherd and his dog, as they guided the sheep into welcoming stables for the long, cold winter.

"Perhaps it's time to go back to the city," he said, as he thought of his warm home, a fire burning in the hearth. So he packed his bags and set off for Venice.

Soon he was in the city, walking over bridges, watching the boats on the canal. People greeted him and whispered... Look, there's Signore Vivaldi, the great musician!

Antonio smiled. His new composition was almost ready and he hoped it would be his greatest work.

Some days it rained in Venice, cold, needle-sharp drops, but soon it turned back to ice and snow, picking out the details on the decorated palaces and churches, sparkling in the low sunlight. New notes came into Antonio's head – he hummed as he walked, and then… he slipped – and fell!

His music papers were scattered across the ice. He gathered them together, but they were all muddled. At last he returned home to put everything back together.

"And now, how should I finish this music?" he asked himself. "In greys and whites?"

Picking up his violin, he played a few notes… It wasn't quite right, not the music he wanted… "I must have colour!" he said.

But it seemed there was no colour to be found in the white Winter.

At last the year turned and it was time for the Carnival!

The great canal froze over, white gave way to bright feathers and masks, and flowing capes scattered like jewels upon the ice, skating and swirling, a kaleidoscope of colour! Antonio watched the ice-dance, as people skated faster and faster, hoping the ice wouldn't crack!

The air was filled with music and merriment, as Winter's end announced the coming of Spring.

Antonio laughed with joy. "Now I have my ending!" he said to himself, as he looked and listened. "I will finish my work today... I will capture a whole year, four seasons... in music!"

THE SUNKEN CATHEDRAL

*Music by Claude Debussy
after an ancient Breton myth*

Deep under the waves, in the bay of Douarnenez, lies the sunken city of Ys. Its magnificent cathedral is covered in weeds and limpets; fish swim in and out of the towers and crabs gather in the city square. It is said that sometimes, when the tide is low enough, the spires of the cathedral rise up above the waves for a few minutes, and the great bronze bells ring out...

Of course, the city hadn't always been under the sea.

The king of Ys built the city for his daughter, the Princess Dahut. She was his only child, and it was she who begged for a city by the shore, with wide views and the sound of the waves lapping nearby.

The king was warned — don't build too close to the sea, for the storms were wild and the waves high. But since the queen had died, he could refuse Dahut nothing, and so the city was built.

The king reassured everyone by building a high wall around it, with just one gateway. This would keep the waves out, for the gates were only to be opened at low tide, when the great bells of the cathedral rang.

The city prospered and the princess grew in height and beauty, in her windswept, salt-aired home by the sea. The king was determined to keep her safe, and so she was never allowed beyond the city walls. But in time, the sound of the waves and seagulls were not enough to keep her content, and she became restless....

One bright day a handsome knight, dressed in red, came to the city of Ys. As soon as she saw him, Dahut's heart belonged to him.

The red knight visited the city every few weeks, and the princess always went to meet him in secret. He would tell her tales of faraway lands, of cities with no walls, where people could come and go as they wished, and be free.

The princess said nothing about the red knight to her father. But eyes watch and tongues talk. People said the Princess Dahut was cursed, that the knight was the devil in disguise, and that they would bring bad fortune to the city of Ys.

Before long the rumours reached the ears of the king, and one night he followed her. Through the winding streets he went, all the way to the city square. There he saw the princess and the red knight together. He became afraid – perhaps the knight would take his beloved daughter far away, beyond the safe city.

The king sent a message to the guards that the red knight must not be allowed past the city gates again. The princess sat in her tower and wept. She could think of nothing but her handsome knight.

Then, one day, Dahut saw the red knight's ship in the bay. Later, when the castle was in darkness, she tiptoed to her father's room. There was the key, on a chain, around his neck. He slept soundly, so she gently undid the chain, took the key, and slipped it in the pocket of her cape.

She ran barefoot through the streets all the way to the city gates. The guards slept, so she turned the key in the lock and pulled the gates wide open. She didn't notice that dark clouds were gathering, or that the tide was turning....

Inside the castle, the king woke up to hear thunder. He put his hand to his neck, and knew at once the key was gone.

"Sound the alarm!" he called. "Ring the bells!"

The cathedral bells echoed around the bay as the king ran down to the sea wall. But by the time he reached the gates, it was too late – they were wide open, and great waves rushed into the city.

The princess heard the distant bells and felt for the key in her pocket. "Oh, the gates... I forgot!" she cried. "I must return to Ys!"

The king, meanwhile, had leaped upon his horse and galloped out into the wild stormy sea to find his daughter. The wind whipped sea-foam into his eyes as the waves grew higher and higher.

Then he saw her, reaching out to him.

"I'm sorry, Father!" she cried.

But a great wave carried her away, and she was gone. The soft sands shifted, towers began to lean and twist, and by the time the king had galloped to safety, the great city of Ys had been swallowed up by the sea.

Sometimes the king would return to the bay of Douarnenez, to listen out for the bells of the engulfed cathedral, tolling under the sea once more. Some say he has even seen a mermaid who resembles the cursed princess, swimming from tower to tower.

Perhaps she is there still, searching for her red knight.

THE PLANETS

*Music by Gustav Holst,
after Greek and Roman mythology — and Astrology*

*In the sky, amongst the stars
Spinning, turning, shining
The planets turn in harmony
By carefully aligning*

Have you ever looked up at the stars, and wondered about them?

The constellations are filled with the strange creatures of the zodiac, while the gods who lend their names to the planets watch over them. Listen, and we can hear the music and stories of the spheres...

MARS, THE BRINGER OF WAR

Thrumming, drumming, danger coming
An army drawing near
The sound of soldiers marching by
The God of War brings fear

Mars was the Roman God of War, a cold, distant figure, usually shown carrying a spear, uncovered when ready for battle, and covered by a laurel wreath in times of peace.

He is said to be the father of many children, but his twin boys, Romulus and Remus, were the most important. After they were born, their grandfather, King Numitor, cast the twin babies into a river. He was afraid they would steal the throne from him. The boys were found by a she-wolf, who raised them as her cubs until they were rescued by a shepherd...

As adults, the brothers argued and fought over where to build a new city. Romulus won, and founded the city of Rome. Because of this, his father Mars is considered the protector of Rome and guardian of the invincible Roman army.

Representing power and strength, Mars was also a handsome lover, falling for the Goddess of Love herself... Venus.

VENUS, THE BRINGER OF PEACE

A goddess, golden, gleaming, pure
At sunset, from afar
Venus shines in splendour
The majestic Evening Star

Venus was married to Vulcan, the God of Volcanoes, but her greatest love was Mars. In ancient legends it is said that Vulcan caught the lovers in an invisible net, and tried to keep them apart, but Mars and Venus loved each other too much. They had many children, including Harmonia, the Goddess of Harmony, and Cupid – the God of Love.

But Venus could also be vain. One story tells of how a golden apple was given to the gods as a gift for the most beautiful goddess amongst them.

The gods could not agree who deserved the golden apple, so they asked a Trojan prince called Paris to choose between three goddesses, Minerva, Juno and Venus. Determined to win, Venus cheated by offering Paris the most beautiful woman in the world, Helen of Troy, and so Paris gladly gave her the apple.

In astrology, Venus is the planet of love, romance and art. She is the first star to appear in the sky after sunset, which is why she is sometimes called the Evening Star.

MERCURY, THE WINGED MESSENGER

Darting, flashing, sparkling sounds
With wings upon his heels
Mercury is the Messenger
Of Gods and their ideals

Mercury had wings on his heels and his helmet, and he could run and fly faster than any other god. If an urgent message needed to be sent, Mercury was the perfect choice. He was swift, quick-witted, and could interpret and even translate messages. He was the master of communication.

Mercury could also play tricks. He was often sent to guide souls to the Underworld, where people went after they died. The beautiful nymph Larunda, a Daughter of the Rivers, was sent there by Jupiter, because she talked too much. But Mercury fell in love with her on the way and hid her in a forest, so Jupiter wouldn't find out. She gave birth to two children by Mercury, and they became Guardians of the Fields and Hedges.

Mercury is the planet of cleverness, intelligence and wit.

JUPITER, THE BRINGER OF JOLLITY

The Father of the Gods
Brings joy and festive jollity
At festivals he revels in
The pleasures of frivolity

Jupiter was the greatest god of all, a symbol of celebration, festivals and ceremonies. But he could also be violent, the God of the Sky and Thunderbolts! Jupiter could see all that was going on, in heaven and on earth. His children became many of the most famous gods and goddesses, which is why he is called the Father of the Gods.

One day Jupiter saw a handsome youth called Ganymede and wanted to bring him to his palace, up in the clouds of Mount Olympus. So he turned himself into an eagle and carried Ganymede up to the kingdom of the gods, where he became a special kind of servant, called a cup-bearer, to Jupiter.

The cup probably held their favourite drink, Ambrosia, which was said to make humans immortal.

In astrology, Jupiter represents growth, prosperity and good fortune.

SATURN, THE BRINGER OF OLD AGE

The God of Generations
Of passing time and age
Civilised and peaceful
A wise and gentle sage

The god Saturn was considered venerable and wise, and also the greatest teacher amongst the gods. He taught agriculture and farming to the Romans, so they could grow crops and live good, long, healthy lives, and so he is also the God of Sowing Seeds. One of the biggest festivals in Rome is named after him – Saturnalia.

But Saturn could be powerful too. In one story he is warned that he will be overthrown by his own child – so he eats him! But his wife hides their second child. He survived and became the King of the Gods – Jupiter!

Saturn is the planet of time, maturity, and the power of perseverance.

URANUS, THE MAGICIAN

Mysterious and distant
A genius, a magician
Aggressive and all-powerful
A spectacular apparition

Uranus is a fascinating but sometimes fearsome god. His wife was Gaia, the Mother of the Earth, and together they were the parents of the one-eyed giant, Cyclops, and the gigantic Titans, who were full of power. The most famous is Prometheus, who first gave fire to humans.

Some say Uranus is the oldest god of all. The God of the Sky, his birth was shrouded in mystery, and he was in command of elemental forces, and creator of the heavens, which is surely a kind of magic. Imagine creating a universe!

In astrology, the planet Uranus symbolises rebellion, independence and surprise!

NEPTUNE, THE MYSTIC

Lastly, comes the mighty Neptune
The God of Wind and Sea
Swimming in the endless oceans
For all eternity

As God of the Oceans and Storms, Neptune is sometimes seen with a merman's tail, carrying a trident, and most stories about him involve the sea, like the legend of Delphinus...

One day Neptune saw the water nymph Amphitrite dancing, and fell in love with her. She refused to marry him, however, and ran away to hide in the Atlas Mountains. So Neptune sent a dolphin to look for her. The dolphin found Amphitrite and persuaded her to change her mind.

As a reward for finding and returning Amphitrite to him, Neptune immortalised the dolphin in the heavens as the constellation Delphinus, and he made Amphitrite Queen of the Oceans.

He is the planet of spirituality and compassion, of dreams and delusions...

So the planets slowly turn
With the stars or sun or moon
And dance their destined patterns
In harmony, in tune

Eternity is their companion
Infinity, their friend
The music of the spheres continues
And echoes, without end...

THE BUTTERFLY LOVERS

*Music by He Zhanhao and Chen Gang
after an ancient Chinese legend*

Almost a thousand years ago, in China, there lived a young girl called Zhu Yingtai. She grew up with her family, in a beautiful house surrounded by peach blossom and willow trees, with pavilions, bridges and ponds full of golden fish. Yingtai had everything she wished for – except for one thing. She longed to go away to be educated.

"It is impossible, only boys go to the college," said her father. "Girls are forbidden."

"I could wear my brother's clothes," said Yingtai, clasping her hands. "If I dress like a boy, will you let me go? I will be careful, I promise you."

Hearing this, her parents agreed, and the next day Yingtai tied up her hair and began to live as a boy. Her parents were astonished to see her look so different, as they bade her farewell.

It was a long way to the college and after two days of walking, Yingtai reached a crossroads. There, she saw a handsome young boy about her age.

"Excuse me," said Yingtai, with her head bowed. "Which is the road to the college?"

"I'm going there myself!" said the boy. "I am Liang Shanbo. Allow me to show you the way."

On the journey, they talked without pause.

"I was born on the seventh day of the seventh moon," said Shanbo. "I am seventeen years old."

"I was born on the same day of the same moon," said Yingtai. "A year after you."

"Then we are almost brothers!" said Shanbo.

Yingtai blushed and smiled. Shanbo felt a strange warmth in his heart for this younger boy.

One night, under the moon, they made a solemn promise – they became sworn-brothers, inseparable and undividable.

Eventually they crossed the Qiantang River to where the college of Hangzhou stood. The master, Confucius, welcomed them, gave the two sworn-brothers a shared room and allowed them to sit together in class. So they began their studies of the literary arts.

Summer came, but even in the heat Yingtai kept herself fully clothed, to be sure no one guessed her secret. Autumn passed and then Winter, when the jasmine began to flower. The two sworn-brothers grew closer and closer.

Yingtai's heart danced to see Shanbo's smile; Shanbo couldn't understand the deep love he felt for this younger sworn-brother, Yingtai. Both studied hard, philosophy and poetry, each determined to be the best they could. They wrote beautiful poems to each other.

But every spring, the peach blossoms reminded Yingtai of home, and after three years she went to the master and knelt before him.

"Thank you, teacher, for your generous wisdom, but I wish to take my leave and return home. My parents are old, and I miss them."

Next, Yingtai went to tell Shanbo, who began to weep at her news.

"Come and visit me," said Yingtai.

"My dear sworn-brother," he cried. "One day I will."

Yingtai embraced Shanbo tightly, and neither wanted to let go. But at last she turned around and walked away.

Yingtai was welcomed by her family, and she told them all about her studies and the honour of being taught by a great master. But she said nothing about Shanbo.

Her parents wasted no time to arrange a marriage. A matchmaker knew a boy who would be a fine husband for beautiful Yingtai. Red silk was embroidered for a wedding gown, and Yingtai wept to think she was betraying the bond between herself and Shanbo. Yet he only thought of her as a brother... and she had to respect her parents' wishes.

So she went sadly to her room and let down her beautiful dark hair, put on fragrance, painted her eyebrows like willow leaves, and dressed in flowery brocade; she was as beautiful as a peony.

Far away, in Hangzhou, Shanbo barely ate or slept, and his heart ached. In the end he went to see the master and explained he needed to visit Yingtai, and would be gone a few weeks.

After several days of walking he reached Yingtai's house, covered in peach blossom, where a beautiful young woman, with a face as pale as the moon, came to the door. Shanbo thought she must be Yingtai's sister…

"I have come to see my sworn-brother, from college, if you please," he said, bowing.

Yingtai smiled. "Dear Shanbo, do you not know me?"

Suddenly Shanbo saw it was his sworn-brother – a beautiful woman! Now his aching heart made sense! He fell on his knees, confessed his great love, and begged Yingtai to be his bride.

"Oh, Shanbo, you are too late!" sighed Yingtai. "I am already betrothed…"

"But we made a bond," said Shanbo.

"As brothers…" said Yingtai.

Shanbo felt his heart was breaking, like the branch of a tree in a storm. He turned and ran. He didn't stop until he reached his parents' house.

There were no peach blossoms there, it was the simple house of a poor family. But it was home, and he told his mother and father all that had happened.

His mother at once set off for Yingtai's home. When she arrived she saw the luxury that Yingtai lived in. Nevertheless, she knelt down to ask her to consider Shanbo's proposal.

Tearfully, Yingtai bowed and explained that she could never disobey her parents, who had already arranged a marriage. She wrote a letter to Shanbo, which said:

My path has been chosen; we cannot marry in this life...

Shanbo's mother took the letter to her son, who read it in silence. He was weak and pale, not eating, heart still breaking. He wept until his eyes closed. They never opened again, for he died that evening.

When Yingtai heard this news, it was her wedding day and she wore the red silk dress. Tears poured from her eyes like pearls, as the wedding procession wound its way along the road.

Suddenly the sky grew dark and a wild storm blew, with whirling winds that threw all the guests to the ground. Yingtai saw they were beside Liang Shanbo's tomb!

She ran to the tomb and knelt down.

"My Shanbo, you know my heart is yours," she wept. "You have reached the Yellow Springs . When I reach there too, I will be your bride."

At her words, a great bolt of lightning struck the tomb, splitting the ground apart. Yingtai saw the ground open before her, and she jumped in with a great cry.

The storm ended as suddenly as it had started. The ground closed up and the sun returned to fill the sky with warmth and light. Then, as the wedding guests stood and watched in astonishment, two exquisite butterflies rose from the tomb.

Up, up they flew, delicately dancing in the air, higher and higher, towards the sun – the souls of true lovers, together for eternity.

For a sworn bond of love that is predestined in one life cannot be broken in the next.

THE FIREBIRD

*Music by Igor Stravinsky
after a Russian folktale*

In the gloom of the long night, something gleamed in the distance. It caught the eye of young Prince Ivan, who had been hunting in the forest and was now lost. The light seemed to be on the other side of a high stone wall.

Ivan tried the gates, but they were locked, so he climbed over the wall and found himself in a garden that glistened and sparkled. The grass was full of delicate, jewel-like flowers, while in the centre there stood an apple tree, laden with golden fruits.

A flickering flame in the dark sky grew bigger and brighter as it flew downwards. It was an extraordinary bird, with feathers of fire! She filled the garden with a dazzling light as she darted through the branches of the tree, eating golden apples.

Ivan hid in the shadows and watched. Then he slowly lifted his crossbow and fired an arrow... but missed. He readied the crossbow for another shot, then hesitated. Perhaps he could capture the bird alive? Carefully he crept up behind the fabulous creature, and wrapped his arms around her.

The Firebird fluttered furiously, but in Ivan's gentle embrace she grew calm, her shimmering flames ever changing from red, to yellow, to gold. Then she spoke...

"Prince, harm me not, and I will give you a gift."

She plucked a feather from her tail and offered it to Ivan. "This

feather is my promise to you. Set me free, and I will return to help you if you are ever in need."

Ivan took the feather. It still flared like a flame, yet it did not burn. Putting it inside his jacket to keep it safe, he released the Firebird.

"Thank you, Prince, you have chosen wisely. My freedom will be your salvation." And glowing brightly, she flew away into the inky night and disappeared.

Ivan was about to leave when, from a dark, distant castle, twelve beautiful princesses appeared, running upon the grass. They found fallen fruits and began throwing them to each other, before joining hands in a round dance beneath the golden apple tree. Just then, a thirteenth princess ran over to them. But she stopped suddenly when she saw the prince.

Ivan bowed to her, captivated by her beauty.

"I am the Tsarevna," she said. "And I implore you, do not linger here. This is the garden of the sorcerer Koschei the Deathless, and we are his prisoners."

"Then I will help you escape," Ivan replied.

"No one knows the secret to his power!" said the Tsarevna. "Stay, and his minions and monsters will capture you, and Koschei will turn you into stone."

Ivan looked around and saw several contorted rocks, once brave young heroes, barely visible in the overgrown gardens, and he knew the Tsarevna spoke the truth. But now a strange sound echoed in the night air. Someone was approaching and the frightened princesses ran to hide.

The huge gates swung open, hideous cobwebby creatures and grotesque animals clambered all around Ivan and held him tight as the great gates closed again. He was trapped.

A tall shadow fell upon Ivan. He looked up to see a figure, bent over with age, more a skeleton than a man. His robes were tatters and he stank of decay. His fingers, like talons, pointed at Ivan. It was Koschei the Deathless!

He leant in very close until Ivan could feel his breath on his face. "Prince, boy, hero – I know your desire – to take away my princesses! You shall not have them. You shall become stone!" He raised his hands and spoke strange magic to transform Ivan.

The thirteen princesses came running from the shadows. The Tsarevna threw herself at Koschei's feet and begged him to show mercy. But Koschei only laughed and continued casting his spell.

Ivan slipped his hand inside his jacket and took out the glowing, golden feather.

"Oh, Firebird, you made me a promise! Now is the time to keep it... please, help me!"

Immediately, the Firebird appeared, a flash of flickering fire. She flew around Koschei and his creatures, leading them in a fast and furious dance, a blaze of sound and flame until, with a crash, they fell to the ground, exhausted.

The Firebird's song became a lullaby, and now, as the garden slept, she led Ivan over to an opening in the roots of a tree.

"My kind prince, listen. Here you will find a casket. Inside is the secret of Koschei's magic – his soul!"

Ivan lifted the casket from the tree roots and opened it. A glowing, golden egg lay inside.

"Take it," said the Firebird.

Ivan gently lifted up the egg.

The garden slowly awoke... and Koschei cried out, "My soul! Give me back my soul!"

Ivan realised he now had power over the evil sorcerer, and he lifted the egg high above his head. It seemed time stood still. Then...

CRASH!

He threw the egg down. Darkness descended and the old castle and garden vanished. Koschei and his magic were destroyed at last.

In the distance, the horizon glowed and Ivan saw that the stone figures were restored to men –twelve heroes, each with a princess by his side.

The Tsarevna came and took his hand as the great gates swung open.

"Let us leave this terrible place," said Ivan. They stepped towards the rising sun, through the forest, until they came to a glittering golden palace.

"My Tsarevna," said the prince. "Welcome to my kingdom. Will you will be my queen?"

The Tsarevna gazed upon his kind face. "Of course, my love," she said. "A new dawn awaits!"

Above them something gleamed brighter even than the sun... the Firebird!

Ivan bowed in gratitude – and in a blaze of iridescent sparks and flame – she was gone!

MUSICAL NOTES FROM THE AUTHOR

Find out about the composers, the writers who inspired them, the stories and the music. There are also recommended recordings of the music to stream or download.

The Carnival of the Animals by Camille Saint-Saëns (1835-1921)

This is such a popular and famous work, it's hard to believe the composer banned it from public performance in his lifetime – he thought it was too funny for a serious and important composer! After a private performance in 1886 it wasn't heard again until 1922. It then became famous all over the world.

It is scored for a very small chamber ensemble of just twelve instruments, including two pianos. There isn't a story as such; instead it is a collection of short pieces of music describing many different animals. Lots of writers have written poems or stories about these animals. Saint-Saëns uses the word 'carnival', and I imagined a festive parade, introduced by the king of the animals – the lion. The verses I've written about the animals are adapted from those I've used in live performances. They are a bit like riddles.

Saint-Saëns included lots of little jokes in his music. The Tortoise moves to a very slow can-can (a famous dance from Paris, by another composer, Jacques Offenbach), while the Characters With Long Ears sound like donkeys, but some people think Saint-Saëns was making fun of critics, who had been unkind about his music. Some animals have particular instruments to represent them, like the glockenspiel for Fossils, sounding a bit like bones rattling, or the ethereal glass harmonica in Aquarium and the beautiful cello solo for The Swan. I wonder which animal is your favourite?

The Four Seasons by Antonio Vivaldi (1678-1741)

This is undoubtedly Antonio Vivaldi's most famous music, loved and known all over the world. It is also considered one the very earliest pieces of programmatic or story music.

Vivaldi was not only a brilliant composer, he was also a superb violinist, and a Catholic priest, ordained in 1703. On account of his red hair, he was sometimes known as The Red Priest. Although he lived much of his life in Venice, where he was born, in 1718 he was given an important job in Mantua, as director of music for the Governor. Inspired by the countryside there, he wrote four violin concertos – works for solo violin accompanied by an ensemble of other string players and a harpsichord. This became his masterpiece, *The Four Seasons.* It was considered revolutionary, for not only was the music dazzlingly clever, it is believed that Vivaldi based it on poems of his own, describing the passing seasons in the countryside.

Each "season" or concerto has three sections, and within the musical score Vivaldi did something truly unique - bar by bar he wrote descriptions of what the music represented: bubbling brooks, spring breezes, summer storms, birdsong, barking dogs, buzzing bugs, weeping shepherds, hunters' horns and skaters on the ice. The composer's own words inspired my retelling, in which I've imagined Vivaldi watching the seasons unfold throughout a year.

The Sunken Cathedral by Claude Debussy (1862-1918)

Debussy is sometimes called an 'impressionistic' composer. Like the French painters of the time, he tried to capture atmospheric moments in colourful music. What could be more atmospheric than a sunken city?

Originally this was one of a collection of 'preludes' written for solo piano. It was so astonishingly beautiful that several other composers decided to arrange it for a full orchestra. They include Leopold Stokowski, Sir Henry Wood and Colin Matthews.

The Breton legend of the city of Ys, sometimes called Ker-is, first appears in stories as long ago as the 15th century. Over time, the stories have grown and changed, and there are many different versions. I've focused on the story of the princess and the destruction of the great city. In the music, Debussy doesn't tell the whole tale. He describes the cathedral some years after it had sunk, when the bells still rang solemnly under the waves, and at low tide the spires appeared above the water for a few moments. It's really like an illustration in music, yet it captures the drama and sadness of the whole story.

When you listen to the music, perhaps you will hear bells, deep under the sea...

The Planets by Gustav Holst (1874-1934)

Gustav Holst was a British composer, and this suite was inspired by Astrology – how the constellations and planets might affect our fortunes. Rather than depicting Zodiac signs, Holst chose to focus on the planets, taking their astrological characteristics as his starting point. The first complete performance was given in 1920.

Tales of the Roman gods are mostly adapted from earlier Greek mythology. They are full of a kind of magic and curious incidents that seem very strange to us today, but the Romans believed these gods existed and affected their lives. They named the planets after their most important gods, and Holst's music describes their individual qualities.

When Holst wrote his music, just after World War I, he was also influenced by the reality of the changing world around him. It is easy to hear the fear and terror in *Mars: the Bringer of War*. It is notable that he chose to describe Venus as the Bringer of Peace, not the Goddess of Love. The most famous piece is perhaps *Jupiter*, for it was adapted by Holst himself for Cecil Spring-Rice's patriotic hymn, *I Vow To Thee My Country*.

The suite of seven planets uses a huge orchestra, dazzling us with extraordinary sounds, from the brass and drums in *Mars*, to the shimmering strings in *Venus*, the percussion for *Mercury* and great tubular bells for *Uranus*. The music transports us far away, to other timeless worlds of myth and legend, as well as the far reaches of our solar system. It ends with an extraordinary representation of infinity, as a wordless female chorus fades slowly away into nothing...

The Butterfly Lovers by He Zhanhao (born 1933) & Chen Gang (born 1935)

This beautiful work is very much loved throughout China and Asia. Chinese composers He Zhanhao and Chen Gang wrote the work together, as students, and like *The Four Seasons*, it is a violin concerto, for a solo violinist and an orchestra. The music skilfully blends traditional Chinese sounds and melodies for a Western orchestra, and it's a deeply moving and tender musical retelling of this famous Chinese legend.

Sometimes called *Liang Shanbo* after one of the lovers in the story, it is also known as a Chinese *Romeo and Juliet*. A very ancient tale from the Eastern Jin dynasty of China (AD 317 to 420), it has inspired paintings, sculptures, and many retellings. *The Butterfly Lovers Concerto* has become especially famous.

The solo violin of the concerto is symbolic of Zhu Yingtai, the girl, and the cello part represents Liang Shanbo. Sometimes the solo violin part is played on an erhu – a Chinese two-stringed instrument. One of the melodies comes from a Chinese folk song, *Yellow River*. In Chinese tradition, the Yellow River is the land of the dead.

The exquisite, fragrant music closely follows the story, depicting the emotions of the two characters, from naive young students to heartbroken lovers, and finally two beautiful butterflies.

The Firebird by Igor Stravinsky (1882-1971)

Stravinsky was born in Russia, but he left just before the Russian Revolution. He settled first in Switzerland, then Paris, France, before making the USA his home. He has sometimes been called 'The Father of Modern Music' because after *The Firebird*, he explored more experimental, unusual sounds, and exciting new rhythms.

Originally *The Firebird* was written for a ballet, commissioned by the famous Ballet Russe company. The story is derived from several Russian folk tales and was a sensational success at its premiere, in Paris, in 1910. Audiences loved the spectacular and colourful sets and costumes as much as the music and dancing.

The original ballet is around 50 minutes long, but in 1919, Stravinsky himself arranged a short concert suite of around 20 minutes, to be performed on its own without dancers, and it is in this form the music is most often heard today. Stravinsky arranged several other suites of extracts, and in all versions *The Firebird* is full of beautiful tunes and harmonies. But there are also some strange, magical and often very atmospheric sounds, pointing to his future as an innovator in composition.

The 1919 suite is the best of all the versions, and follows the story scene by scene, beginning with the Prince lost in a gloomy forest. Then follow all the key scenes – the dance of the Firebird, the round dance of the princesses (Stravinsky uses a traditional Russian folk tune), the devilish dance of the sorcerer, Koschei, a lullaby and the magnificent grand finale, with its famous and transcendentally beautiful 'hymn'.

RECOMMENDED RECORDINGS

Find the music for all the pieces in this book on Youtube or stream/download on Spotify or wherever you listen to your music. Here are some great recordings specially recommended by James Mayhew.

The Carnival of the Animals
Cristina Ortiz and Pascal Rogé (piano), London Sinfonietta conducted by Charles Dutoit (Decca)
Martha Argerich and Nelson Freire (piano), Gidon Kremer (violin) (Decca)
Aldo Ciccolini and Alexis Weissenberg (piano), Orchestre de la Société des Concerts du Conservatoire conducted by Georges Prêtre (Erato)

The Four Seasons
Nigel Kennedy (violin & director), English Chamber Orchestra (Warner)
Enrico Onofri (violin) with Il Giardino Armonica directed by Giovanni Antonini (Warner)
Giuliano Carmignola (violin) with the Venice Baroque Orchestra directed by Andrea Marcon (Sony)

The Sunken Cathedral
Sometimes the French title of the music is used, *La Cathédrale Engloutie.*
Debussy arr. Stokowski – New Philharmonia Orchestra conducted by Leopold Stokowski (Decca)
Debussy arr. Stokowski – Philharmonia Orchestra conducted by Geoffrey Simon (Cala)
Debussy arr. Matthews – Hallé Orchestra conducted by Sir Mark Elder (Hallé)

If you'd like to hear the original piano version, there are many recordings by fine pianists like Hélène Grimaud, Pascal Rogé, Krystian Zimmerman, Maurizio Pollini and Daniel Barenboim.

The Planets
Berlin Philharmonic Orchestra conducted by Herbert von Karajan (Deutsche Grammophon)
London Philharmonic Orchestra conducted by Vladimir Jurowski (LPO label)
Orchestre Symphonique de Montréal conducted by Charles Dutoit (Decca)

The Butterfly Lovers
Takako Nishizaki (violin), New Zealand Symphony Orchestra conducted by James Judd (Naxos)
Vanessa-Mae (violin), London Philharmonic Orchestra conducted by Viktor Fedotov (Warner)
Gil Shaham (violin), Singapore Symphony Orchestra conducted by Lan Shui (Canary)

The Firebird
The Philadelphia Orchestra conducted by Riccardo Muti (Warner)
Orchestre de l'Opéra Bastille conducted by Myung-Whun Chung (Deutsche Grammophon)
Baltimore Symphony Orchestra conducted by David Zinman (Telarc)